click
click
click!

For all the well-loved and well-worn toys in the family.
Blah Blah, Lizzie and Pengy, you know who you are!

Published by
PEACHTREE PUBLISHING COMPANY INC.
1700 Chattahoochee Avenue
Atlanta, Georgia 30318-2112
www.peachtree-online.com

Text and illustrations © 2020 by Julia Woolf

First published in Great Britain in 2020 by Andersen Press Ltd.
20 Vauxhall Bridge Road, London, SW1V 2SA
First United States edition published in 2020 by Peachtree Publishing Company Inc.

The illustrations were created with mono printing, hand painted, and then digitally colored in Adobe Photoshop.

Printed in February 2020 in Malaysia
10 9 8 7 6 5 4 3 2 1
First Edition

ISBN: 978-1-68263-201-7

Cataloging-in-Publication Data is available from the Library of Congress

Julia Woolf

Duck & Penguin
Do NOT Like
Sleepovers

PEACHTREE
ATLANTA

This is Betty and Maud. They are best friends and they love spending time together. Especially with their favorite toys, Duck and Penguin...

who aren't so thrilled.

Betty and Maud are excited to have a sleepover.
"But not just any sleepover!" squeals Betty.

"We're going to spend the night together...

in a TENT!"

"A teeny-weeny tiny tent!" shrieks Maud.

"We'll be nice and cozy," says Betty.
"Right next to each other all...night...long!"

Duck and Penguin aren't so sure.

Betty and Maud decide to set up their tent in the garden.

"Pop-up tents are the best," says Betty.

"Just toss them in the air," says Maud, "and—"

"Oh look!" says Betty. "Penguin is flying with the tent!"
"Such a clever penguin," says Maud.

Betty and Maud anchor the tent with pegs
and check that everything is safe and secure.
"The ropes are nice and tight," says Betty.

"Be careful not to trip over them,"
says Maud.

"Oh yes," says Betty.
"Otherwise you could fall over."

Inside the tent, Betty and Maud get ready for bedtime.

"These sleeping bags are so snuggly," says Betty.

"These pillows are supersoft," says Maud. "Duck and Penguin are going to love them!"

While the girls have been inside the tent,
the light has started to fade.

"Oooh," says Betty, "let's get our jammies on."

"Duck and Penguin love wearing their onesies,"
says Maud.

Betty and Maud settle in for
an after-dark snack.

"I love fizzy pop," says Betty.
"It's the best!" says Maud.
"Look how much Duck and Penguin love it too."

Oh dear,
Betty and Maud
drank too much
fizzy pop!

"I need to tinkle,"
says Betty.
"Me too,"
says Maud.

"Let's go back to the house," says Betty.
"Quick!" says Maud. "I can't hold it much longer!"

And off
they run.

Uh-oh. Betty and Maud have left Duck and Penguin behind. Duck and Penguin do not like sleepovers.

Duck and Penguin do not like being in the teeny-weeny tiny tent.

Duck and Penguin have decided to go back to the house too.

snort, snuffle

Skittle, scuttle

Outside, there are lots of
strange noises.

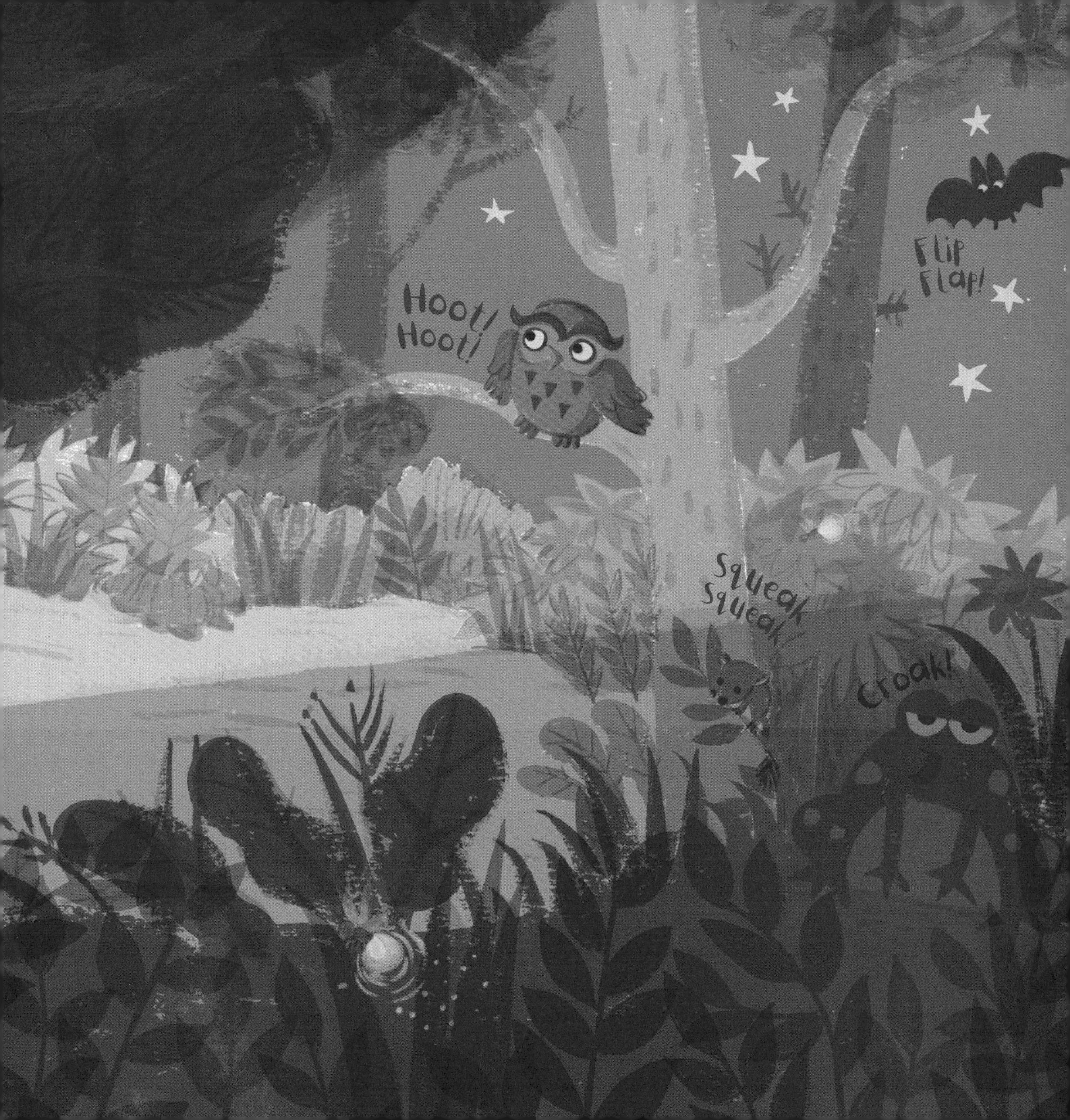
Hoot! Hoot!
Flip Flap!
Squeak Squeak
Croak!

Duck and Penguin do not like strange noises

or the dark outside

or creepy crawlies.

And they're having trouble finding the house.

Duck and Penguin
have the feeling...

that something is watching them.

Duck and Penguin think it might be
a good idea to get back to the tent.

Duck and Penguin like being in
the teeny-weeny tiny tent.

After a good night's sleep in a bed
in the house, Betty and Maud
come back to the tent.

"Oh look," says Betty. "Duck and Penguin made a new friend!"

"Kitty Kat has been looking after Duck and Penguin *all* night," says Maud.

"I think Duck and Penguin must have had the best night's sleep ever," says Betty.

"They really, *really* love sleepovers," says Maud.

"In the teeny-weeny tiny tent," says Betty.